FREE:
One Santa Suit

The views expressed within this work are the sole responsibility of the author and do not necessarily reflect the position of Cedar Fort, Inc., or any other entity.

This is a work of fiction. The characters, names, incidents, places, and dialogue are products of the author's imagination, and are not to be construed as real.

ISBN 13: 978-1-59955-431-0

Published by Bonneville Books, an imprint of Cedar Fort, Inc., 2373 W. 700 S., Springville, UT 84663
Distributed by Cedar Fort, Inc., www.cedarfort.com

Library of Congress Cataloging-in-Publication Data

Brown, Shauna V., 1949-
  Free-- one Santa suit / Shauna V. Brown.
    p. cm.
  ISBN 978-1-59955-431-0 (acid-free paper)
  1. Cancer--Patients--Fiction. 2. Sick children--Fiction. 3. Santa Claus--Fiction. I. Title.

PS3602.R72287F74 2010
813'.6--dc22

                                        2010013382

Cover and page design by Tanya Quinlan
Cover design © 2010 by Lyle Mortimer
Edited by Kimiko Christensen Hammari

Printed in Canada

10 9 8 7 6 5 4 3 2 1

Printed on acid-free paper

FREE:
One Santa Suit

Shauna V. Brown

J illian wrote the final words on the classified ad and placed it before the clerk.

"I hope you can read it. My handwriting isn't what it used to be. It's a bit shaky," she said while tears filled her eyes. "This is hard for me."

The clerk smiled. "Let me read it for you, and I'll count the words to make sure it is just the way you want it." Clearing her throat, she read aloud, "One Santa Suit, complete. Handmade, beautiful red velvet, lined, fur trimmed, with belt loops. Santa hat to match, gloves, two pairs of pants with pockets, belt, and boots. Would sell today for over $600. FREE to someone who can fill Santa's boots."

"That's a deal!" the clerk exclaimed. "A six-hundred-dollar suit for FREE?"

"Well," Jillian said, affirming, "it is a beautiful Santa suit. I made it and it took hours and hours of sewing. We even ordered a real beard. It's the perfect outfit." Looking closer at the ad, Jillian asked, "Could you enlarge and make this line bolder? FREE to someone who can fill Santa's boots. That is why my offer is free."

"I'll make it thicker and larger type, but that will cost two dollars more."

"That will be fine. It's more important that I locate someone who truly wants to be a Santa Claus," said Jillian. "Oops, I forgot to put my phone number."

As soon as the next issue of the newspaper ran, the phone began to ring.

1

Jillian's daughter, Tracy, who was visiting, said, "Well, Mother, I bet it's another call for the Santa suit. It's taken you long enough to get rid of it. It has hung in your closet for over four years now."

"Tracy, sometimes . . . it takes a bit of time to let go. I kept it around because it still had a trace of your father within it. I would often go and wrap the coat around my shoulders, breathe in, and retrace those sweet and marvelous memories of him. Oh, how I miss my Santa."

"You call those marvelous moments? How memorable can a kicking and screaming child placed upon a lap be? And too often some of them even left a wet impression on Santa's lap." Tracy smirked.

"That's why I made two pairs of pants," said Jillian. "Yes, there were those moments when I thought your Father might hang up his red and white suit, but each year, for twenty-two years, he put the suit on again. Imagine that. He was drawn back to lift those little ones, listen to their wishes, and for just a moment bring them a dream of possibilities. The good far outweighed the bad, Tracy. Somehow, your father became the perfect jolly old fellow. He brought delight every Christmas season. He was meant to be shared. If he could have been Santa 365 days of the year he would have been."

"I bet that's why Daddy always carried candy in his pockets. He never tired of giving a small bit of joy to the children," Tracy reflected.

There were at least a dozen calls that afternoon regarding the classified ad. One by one Jillian tried to set up times for interviews, only to find most were too busy to

be bothered. In fact, some were just plain irritable and cranky.

"You said it was a free Santa suit, not that I had to audition for the part."

"An interview? Gosh, I don't have time, lady."

" I know I can HO, HO, HO, with the best of them. I'll be your perfect Santa. I only charge fifty-eight dollars an hour. I'm a deal, and I can throw in my wife as an elf."

The next afternoon when Tracy called to check on Jillian and the response to the ad, Jillian said, "I've had at least twenty calls. I thought finding the perfect Santa Claus would be an easy task, but it isn't happening. I'm learning that most of the callers are all about the money."

Jillian was hopeful when John Minson agreed to a personal interview. Jillian eagerly opened the front door. Standing before her stood a man wearing a hospital mask that covered his nose and mouth.

"Don't mind me. This is not a hold-up. I want to be Santa Claus."

Jillian stood wide-eyed as he removed his hat. "You're bald!"

"Gosh, can you believe it?" He chuckled. "All I want for Christmas is hair, so I need a real man's hat to cover my losses. I saw your ad and got a great idea, so here I am at your doorstep."

Noticing Jillian's chagrin and serious face, he continued with a warm and personable voice. "I'd like to try to fill those Santa boots." Standing taller, he affirmed, "You see, I believe I know how children going through cancer treatments feel. Well, lets just say . . . " Clearing his throat, he started to sing a familiar Christmas melody. "They need a little Christmas, right this very minute!"

Jillian stood back, marveling, and found a moment to laugh, as well as find an instant affection for him.

"I believe I'm just who you're looking for. First, my eyes sparkle, and I have a great deep laugh. HO, HO, HO," he bellowed. "Pretty good, huh? I've gained some weight from my treatments, which naturally gives me that little round belly look," he said, giving her a side profile. "Not bad, huh? Most important, I have a desire to make those sick kids a little happier. Take their minds off the treatments. Can you imagine the children when they see Santa with an IV drip dangling from a bag? A bald Santa to boot! Awesome, don't you think? I have to be at the hospital more than not, so why not do something good to pass the time."

Despite the hospital mask, Jillian clearly felt that John just might fill her classified requirement. He was a happy soul in spite of the "little inconvenience," as he put it.

"I can be there day and night—almost an on-call Santa."

"You're it, John Minson, you're my handpicked Santa!" announced Jillian as she placed the large box labeled "Santa Suit" in his hands. "I'll come see you in the hospital, if that's all right."

"Perfect!" he said. "Happy to have everyone come. Come one, come all!" he said eagerly, taking hold of the box.

Several weeks later, as the holiday season began, Jillian invited Tracy to drive her to see their Santa Claus.

4

"So, Mama, you found your perfect Santa, and now we get to check him out, see him in action?" Tracy said. "Which mall is he at?"

"Oh, Tracy, he's not at any mall. He's at St. Joseph's Hospital."

"Cool, to the hospital we go," Tracy said with a smile, "to see our classified Santa Claus."

Standing before the information desk, Jillian said, "We're looking for John Minson."

"What room is he in?" the worker asked.

"Oh, I don't know, but . . ." Bending closer, Jillian whispered, "He's playing Santa Claus."

"Santa? Yes, yes, he's on the third floor, D-wing," the woman said, pointing. "He's the best Santa we've ever had here. The children have all taken to him. It's quite the Christmas." She giggled.

Walking down the hallway, Jillian and Tracy quickly shared smiles as they noted the bright Christmas decorations. "Well, it seems like the holiday spirit is definitely here," said Jillian.

"It's beginning to look a lot like Christmas," Tracy began to sing. "Everywhere!"

Christmas wreaths, snowmen, holly, bells, snowflakes, and candy canes made out of construction paper lined the hallways. Snowflakes had been sprayed on mirrors. They paused as they watched a nurse and a little helper tie a large red bow on a doorknob. Tracy remarked, "Looks like the holiday excitement is bursting all around."

It wasn't long before they could hear Christmas music and the sound of children singing songs. The added sounds of bells jingling made the usually quiet and austere corridors of the hospital come alive.

"Oh, there he is," said Tracy, pointing with bubbling excitement. "Mother, he looks great in Daddy's suit." Then she noticed. "He's got an IV drip, Mom! Gosh, he's sick."

"I know. John has cancer. He felt if he had to be in the hospital for treatments, he might as well be serving a need," Jillian explained. "Isn't that wonderful? These children all have something in common and so does he."

Tracy grew quiet and surveyed the room filled with children. Some wore hospital masks, some were in pajamas and robes, and some were in hospital gowns. Some wore bandanas around their heads, and some were bald. Some had IV bags, while others were in wheelchairs. A few were even lying in their beds. A woman wearing a pink jacket was passing out striped beanies. Tables had been set up and filled with stacks of red and green construction paper, glue, pompoms, and glitter. Santa was all decked out in a green Queen Anne's chair at the end of the huge room. Above his chair a large sign read: "Santa's Workshop of Love."

Jillian smiled. "How cute is that? Santa's Workshop of Love. Your father would have thought that was just about the best."

Nurses were pushing wheelchairs to the area made just for Santa and his helpers. Santa sat with a microphone so everyone could hear. Children surrounded the tables and were busy gluing and cutting. Scissors were actively following patterns, and parents and nurses assisted some of the children. The room was a flurry of holiday excitement.

"Come on in, you're just in time to help!" bellowed a familiar voice over the microphone. "Santa can't do all this alone. Look at all my helpers," he said, pointing at his vast and varied crew. "We've got lots of people in this hospital to bring some holiday joy and hope to," he said. "We're making decorations to put in every room in the hospital, and that's three hundred and twenty rooms. We're also making Christmas cards for the soldiers in Iraq."

Eight-year-old Jed saw the pair standing in the doorway and waved them over. "You can sit by me and glue."

Noticing his red and white striped beanie, Tracy commented, "You look like one of Santa's elves."

"Cool, huh? Some women at a league made them for us. I don't have any hair left, and it keeps my head warm."

"Well, those ladies must have been busy knitting. There's got to be at least one hundred of those beanies," said Jillian, sitting across the table. "You really do look like Santa's helper."

"We want to be," said Jed. "Santa told us that our Christmas is better when we think of others, and the pain won't be as bad. Santa brought in cases and cases of paper, glue, and stuff. It's so awesome. He's bald too, just like me."

For weeks Santa stayed with the children in his Workshop of Love and made the hospital a better place. Jillian delighted in each visit as she observed her handpicked Santa Claus offering comfort, hope, and a bright spark of the Christmas spirit.

Jillian was amazed when the head nurse told her, "Even in the middle of the night

7

he has donned the suit and visited a child who just couldn't get to sleep or was in such pain that he needed some comfort. He's truly more like a Christmas angel than Santa Claus." She then continued, "He told me about your ad in the newspaper for the free Santa suit. He has commented over and over that he has loved every minute of playing Santa, although I must admit, I don't know how he does it all. He has an undying will to give, as well as an undying will to live. He just keeps saying, 'Bringing an ounce of joy is my medicine, and it helps me to make it through another day.' "

Jillian smiled. "Oh, I knew the moment I met him. John came to my home with his hospital mask and bald head. I was a bit taken aback by it, but this has been a wonderful experience watching him step into that Santa suit. Never in my wildest dreams did I think filling Santa's boots could be so delightful. I'm sure my Robert would be pleased."

Later that evening, Jillian and Tracy sat on the couch in Jillian's living room and flipped through the pages of a large photo album.

"Oh, I think he's going to love it," Jillian said. "Pictures of the children, the Workshop of Love. I like this one of John dressed from tip to toe as Santa Claus."

"Look, there he is with the hospital mask and his IV drip," Tracy said. "He's still holding the children on his lap, even with the IV."

"He looks a bit tired in this picture," said Tracy, "but he's like the Energizer bunny that just keeps going."

They giggled as they thumbed through the pages. "This has been the best Christmas in years for me!" proclaimed Jillian. "I know those children have had a marvelous

8

Christmas because of John. I think he'll appreciate this book and all the pictures."

On Christmas Day, Jillian and Tracy drove to the hospital. After Tracy routinely pushed the button to the third floor, Jillian fluffed up the bow on the beautifully wrapped package. "I can hardly wait for John to see it," Jillian said in almost childlike anticipation.

They exited the elevator and saw all the decorations hung in the halls. Tracy remarked that it was evident that Santa's workshop had completed its quest while bringing the holiday spirit to hundreds. But when they knocked on John's door, he did not answer. Instead, the head nurse, Margaret, opened the door slowly. "Oh, I knew you would come." She motioned them to enter. Instantly Jillian and Tracy both felt a solid stillness and like they were staring at a huge empty page. The bed was newly made, and upon it lay the red velvet Santa suit. The hat and gloves were folded neatly on top. The tall black boots remained on the floor beside the bed.

Margaret wiped her eyes and said, "I've watched hundreds of people pass away, but somehow he was different. He made it all the way to Christmas. Last night he walked the halls, yelling out to everyone on the floor, 'Merry Christmas to all, and to all a good night.' And then, about two o'clock this morning, he just faded away." Margaret's voice cracked with emotion, "Everybody loved him. He made such a difference." Stepping closer to the side table, Margaret picked up an envelope. "He left you a note," she said quietly and placed it in Jillian's hands.

Visibly shaken and with tears surfacing, Jillian spoke. "I can't read without my glasses. Tracy, could you please read it?"

9

Tracy's face reflected the loss as she sat down on the chair by the bed and read aloud:

Dear Jillian,

HO! HO! HO! It was my best Christmas ever! I'm glad I found your classified ad. Your Santa suit may have been free, but to me it was priceless. It was indeed an honor to wear your handmade Santa suit. I can understand why your Robert enjoyed playing the part of Santa Claus. Because of it, I'm sure I held onto life just a little longer. The doctors told me it would be a miracle to make it to Thanksgiving. Well, we surprised them, didn't we? I even surprised myself. Perhaps it's because your suit allowed me to love a little more, give just a few more squeezes in life, bring more hope to some, a kind word to another, a dream of possibilities.

I may not have looked the part of the perfect Santa, me being bald, but what a blessing! It allowed me to see my family a few more days, hug my sweetheart a few more weeks, and thank my Heavenly Father for the miracle of life—every day. I loved every moment of it.

Regretfully, Jillian, I believe I won't be able to wear the Santa suit again. I am hopeful that you will find another person who needs and wants to bring a little joy to the holiday season. I tried to fill those big black boots as best I could.

Your red velvet suit was a blessing to me and hundreds of others. May you have a very Merry Christmas!

Warmly,

John Minson

Your handpicked Santa Claus

P. S. I can hardly wait to meet your Robert!

ABOUT THE AUTHOR

Graduating from Brigham Young University with a degree in speech and drama has provided Shauna V. Brown with many opportunities to write and direct original plays and presentations for church and community groups. Over the past fifteen years, she has shared her musical talents with original scripts and resources for LDS pioneer trek groups now numbering in the hundreds. Shauna has also enjoyed being a presenter at BYU Education Week and women's conferences.

Shauna and her husband, Rick, have been blessed with six children and ten grandchildren. For the past nineteen years, Shauna has written an original Christmas story as a gift to neighbors and friends.